W9-BQI-374

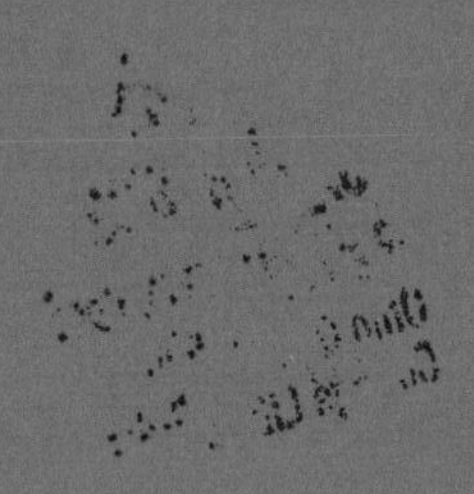

GRAMPS and the FIRE DRAGON

by Bethany Roberts • illustrated by Melissa Iwai

Clarion Books • New York

Clarion Books
a Houghton Mifflin Company imprint
215 Park Avenue South, New York, NY 10003

The illustrations for this book were executed in acrylic and oil paints.
The type was set in 19-point Clearface.

Printed in Hong Kong.

Library of Congress Cataloging-in-Publication Data

Roberts, Bethany. Gramps and the fire dragon / by Bethany Roberts
p. cm.
Summary: Jesse and Gramps aren't sleepy, so they sit in front of the fire and talk
about the beautiful and scary things they see in its flames.
ISBN 0-395-69849-9
[1. Fire—Fiction. 2. Grandfathers—Fiction. 3. Bedtime—Fiction.
4. Imagination—Fiction.] II. Title.
PZ7.R5396Gr 1996
[E]—dc20 94-43097
CIP
AC

SCP 10 9 8 7 6 5 4 3 2

To the real Gramps and Nana, with love
—B.R.

For Bob and Joan
—M.I.

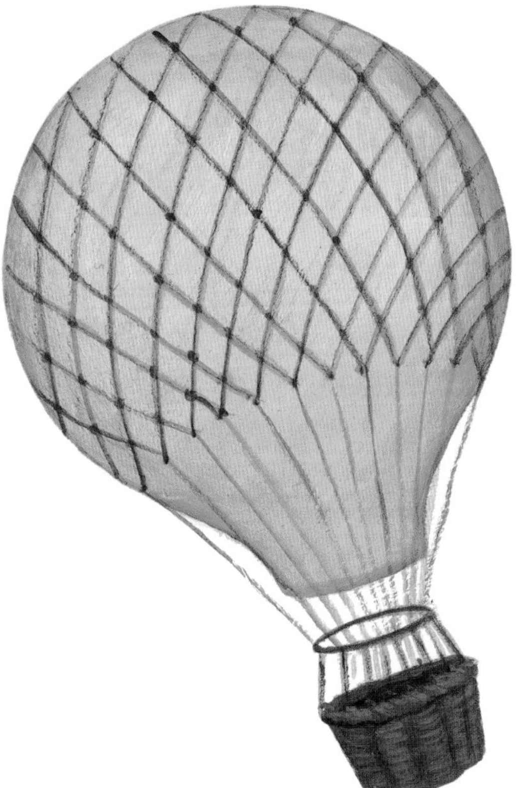

It's bedtime," said Jesse.
"But I'm not sleepy."
"Me neither," said Gramps.

And they rocked in front of the fire,
back and forth,
back and forth.

ADVENTURES
in the
AMAZON

"Look into the fire," said Gramps.
"Can you see pictures?
I can see an old twisted apple tree."
"Me, too," said Jesse.

Together, they saw a flower garden,
and a path leading to a castle.

And then—

—they saw a fire dragon.
"Yipes!" cried Jesse.
The fire dragon roared
and began to chase them,
down the path,
through the flower garden,
and up the tree!

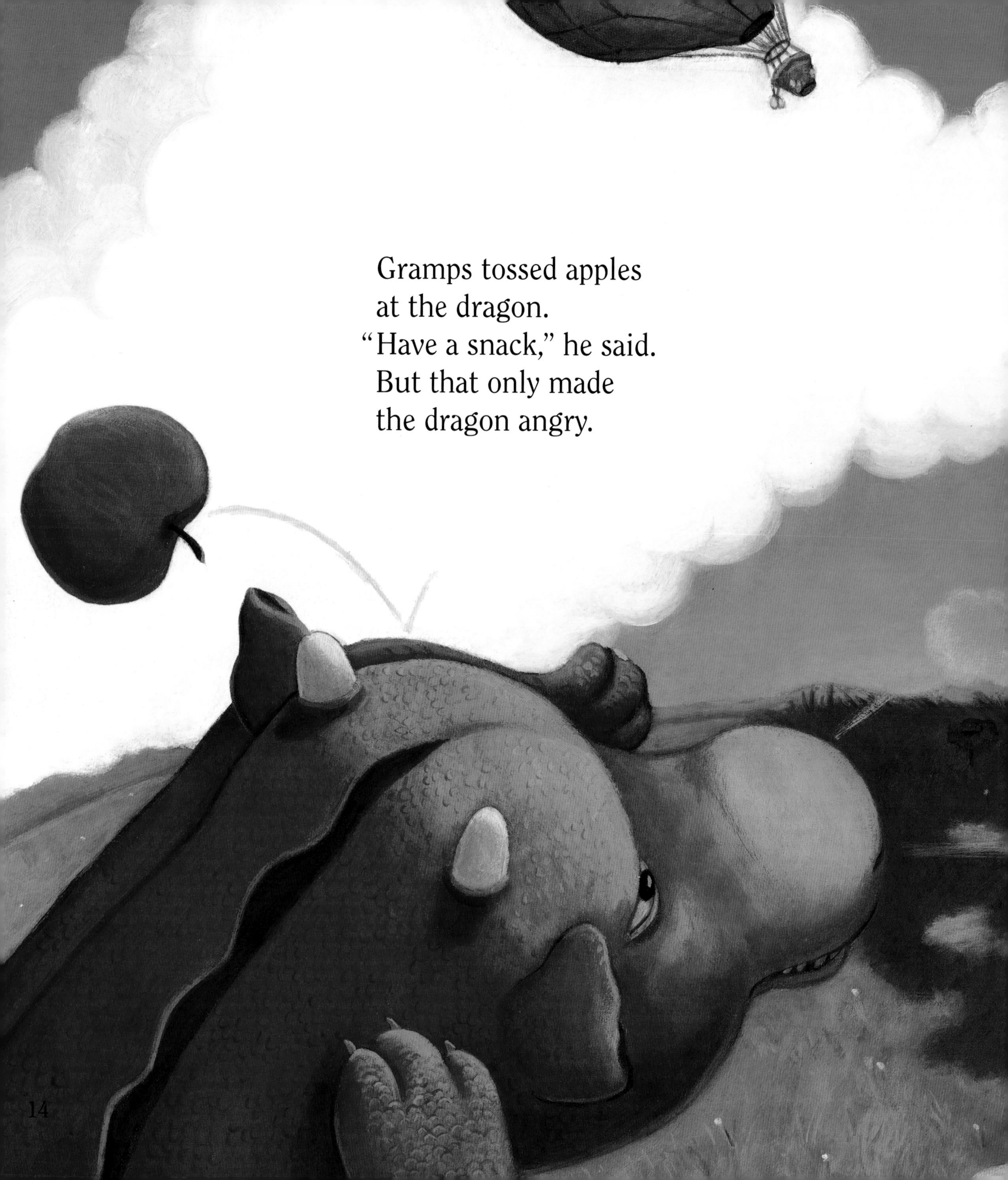

Gramps tossed apples
at the dragon.
"Have a snack," he said.
But that only made
the dragon angry.

Gramps and Jesse hitched a ride
on a passing hot-air balloon.
With a roar, the dragon followed.

Jesse and Gramps zipped down a high mountain.
The dragon zipped, too.

They raced through a jungle.
The dragon raced, too.

They crossed a wide river.
The dragon crossed, too.

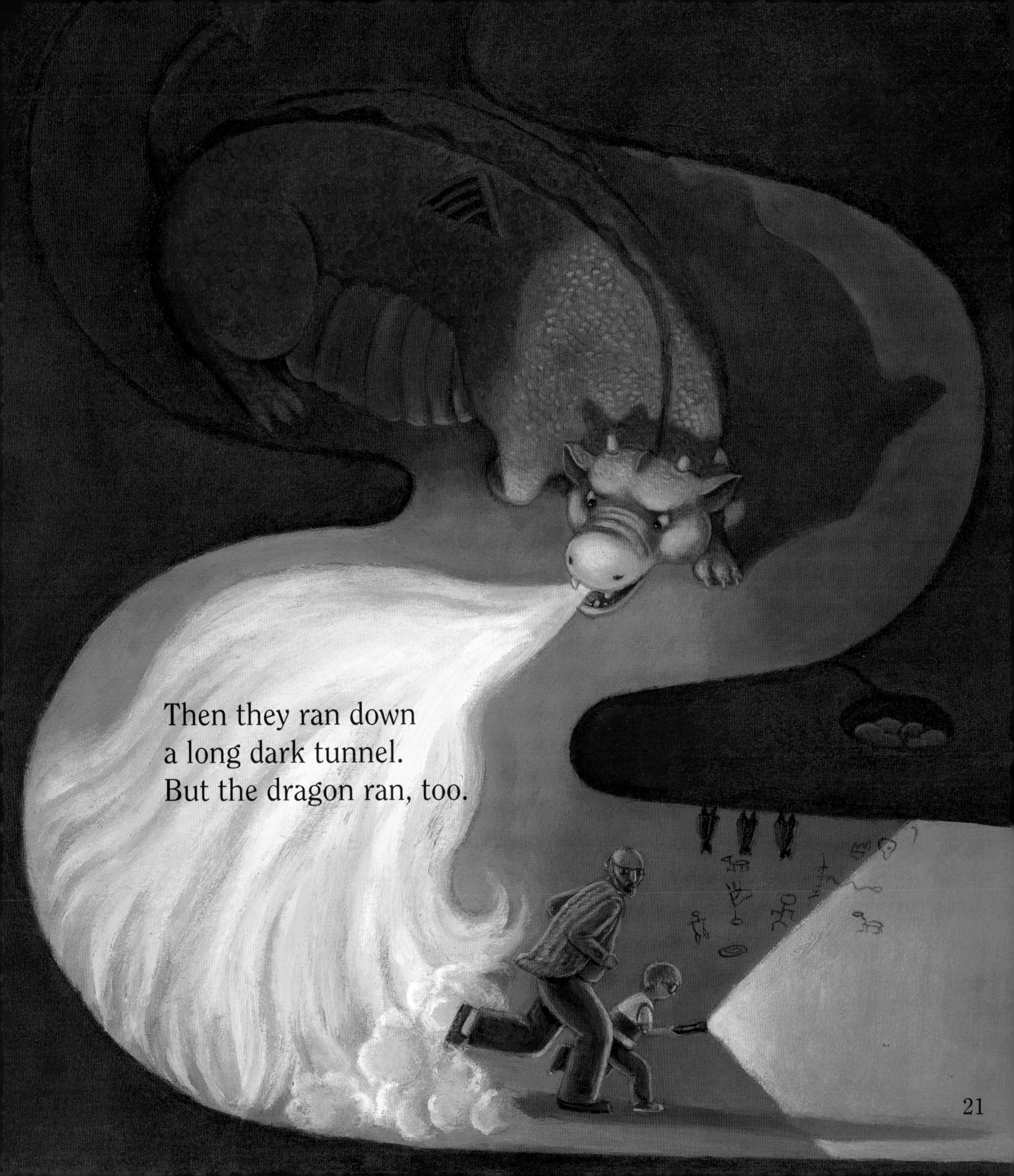

Then they ran down
a long dark tunnel.
But the dragon ran, too.

The dragon was so close,
his flames licked Jesse's heels.

"Run for your life!"
shouted Gramps.

The dragon turned
toward Gramps.

SNAP!

"I'll save you, Gramps!" cried Jesse.
Quickly, he flagged down a fire truck.

Jesse grabbed a hose and sprayed the dragon.

The dragon got smaller,

and smaller,

and smaller,

until there was no dragon at all.

"Just embers left," said Gramps, looking into the fire.

"I guess I saved you, then," said Jesse.
"You sure did," said Gramps.

Gramps yawned.
Jesse yawned.
Then they rocked in front of the fire,
back and forth,
back and forth,

until they fell asleep,
together.